Beth—
Enjoy Mr. Brittany!

Strictly
OFF LIMITS

JESSICA
HAWKINS

D1713766

Strictly Off Limits
A FORBIDDEN ROMANCE NOVELLA

ISBN: 1508770697
ISBN-13: 978-1508770695

TITLES BY
JESSICA HAWKINS

NIGHT FEVER SERIAL
NIGHT FEVER
NIGHT CALL
NIGHT MOVES

THE CITYSCAPE SERIES
COME UNDONE
COME ALIVE
COME TOGETHER

STRICTLY OFF LIMITS

Strictly Off Limits

A FORBIDDEN ROMANCE NOVELLA

Alexandra James gave up her spring break for an offer she couldn't refuse—a week-long job that would earn her enough money to buy her way out of a broken heart. But if she thought her new boss would let her off easy because he's her father's best friend, she couldn't have been more wrong.

Dean Brittany demands perfection from his employees, but none more so than his new temp, since correcting her mistakes seems to fuel his unexpected attraction to her. Unfortunately for him, eighteen-year-old Alexandra is strictly off limits.

CHAPTER 1

I swiped a finger across my iPhone one last time and looked at the piece of art lit up on the screen. Even in the picture I'd snapped before leaving the store, the dress glowed with thousands of tiny, gold sequins. Its beauty was indescribable. Epic. To die for. Giving up my spring break would be worth it. Yes, it was far too lavish and perfect for a fraternity spring formal, but I didn't care. I had something to prove.

The elevator dinged at the top floor of Brittany Industries. My heart thumped once as the doors slid open to reveal a sprawling office that looked as though it were regularly scrubbed with bleach. This was only temporary, but my palms were clammy regardless. It would be my first real job. These paychecks wouldn't be signed by my parents' neighbors with a smiley face as I balanced their four-year-old against my hip.

Each step farther into the office came with a deep inhalation. In reality, I had nothing to worry about—my new boss, Dean Brittany, was an old family friend. He'd watched me grow up. If my dad had such a thing as a best friend, he would be it.

Directly off the elevator was a platinum-haired receptionist with a low-cut blouse. "June" according to her nameplate. She pointed me in the direction of Dean's office. I passed an empty desk just outside his door, which I assumed would be mine, and knocked lightly. When there was no response, I knocked again.

"Come in."

The sunny, downtown Los Angeles skyline brightened an expansive office. Dean was on the phone, his seat angled toward the view so I could only see his profile. He checked his watch and, still staring out the window, motioned for me to sit. I perched on the edge of a chair in front of his desk. He didn't glance at me once as he spoke into the phone. I, on the other hand, had nowhere to look but at him. Since I'd last seen him, his hair had shaded from black to charcoal.

As he listened, his thick eyebrows furrowed until one shot up. "Next month?" he asked. "That'll drive up the cost by thousands. What makes you think I have that to spare?" He paused again, staring out at the skyscrapers. "I'll give you until the end of next week. If it's not finished by then, you can spend *next month* looking for a new job."

He reached out and dropped the receiver without looking, but it landed directly in its cradle.

After a few moments of silence, I spoke. "Dean?"

His leather chair squeaked when he turned to me. "Alexandra James."

His deep voice rolled over my long, mouthful-of-a-name. My friends and family always shortened it to Alex, and it tied my tongue to hear him say it that way—as if it were some risqué inside joke between us. I tucked a loose strand of hair behind my ear.

He stood and came around the desk toward me. In his sharp, navy suit, he wasn't a family friend who used to come over for golf. He wasn't Vivian's dad, the girl I was sometimes forced to play with during dinner parties. The way he leaned in and straightened his jacket before settling against the edge of his desk was almost threatening.

"How long has it been?" he asked. My eyes jumped to meet his. *Those* I remembered—his bottomless eyes. Their deep, dark blue was how I imagined the bottom of the ocean.

"A few years," I said, but it came out like a question.

"Five."

"Oh. Already?"

"That's when I moved to Los Angeles full time. I suppose it's been that long since I've seen you and your mother. How are you liking USC?"

"It's fun," was all I could think to say. I dried my palms against my pants. This was the same Dean I'd grown up around, but my stomach hadn't been this knotted since my first day of classes.

"Good," he said. "I appreciate you doing me this favor. I'm sure this isn't how you imagined spending your first spring break."

"I don't mind," I said. "You're actually doing *me* the favor. I need the extra cash."

"That so?" he asked, shifting against the desk. His knee ghosted against mine, and I jumped a little.

He looked at me expectantly, so I kept talking. "There's this dress…"

He chuckled. "There's always a dress. You sound like Vivian."

"I've been invited to a fraternity formal."

Dean glanced at my hands as I played with the fabric of my pants. I stopped immediately. He still didn't speak.

"It's next weekend," I continued, "and I need a dress for it."

"Won't Gary buy it for you?"

"Normally, yes. But Dad said this one was too much. I believe the word he used was *astronomical*."

He nodded knowingly. "How much is it?"

"Nine hundred and sixty-five dollars. Including tax."

That heavy, dark eyebrow arched again. "For a *frat party*?"

Inside I cringed, but for some reason, my hands dug into my purse for my phone. Dean leaned over when I pulled up the picture, and I caught a hint of his cologne with my inhale.

He made a noise of approval. "I don't know much about fashion," he said, "but as far as dresses go, that's a very nice one. And I imagine you'd look very nice in it."

It was a harmless compliment, but his voice deepened as he said it. I tugged on the ends of my long, light hair. 'Thank you' would've been an appropriate response, but my vocal chords wouldn't cooperate. I was too busy trying not to imagine Dean imagining me in that dress.

"I'm not sure how much Gary told you," he said, "but my secretary, Grace, is out for her honeymoon. She's very good at her job, and without her, my life feels a bit chaotic. I understand this is just a temp thing for you, however, I run a multi-million dollar business. While you're here, you're not Gary's daughter. You're my secretary. Can you handle that?"

"Yes, Dean."

"Mr. Brittany," he corrected immediately. "That's what all my employees call me."

"Yes, Mr. Brittany," I said with a hint of a smile. I'd never addressed any of my parents' friends that way. I doubted I'd be able to do it the entire week.

His eyes searched mine, and he cleared his throat. "Very good. You seem to take direction well. If that's true, we should have no problems."

"Consider me yours for the next five days," I quipped. "I'll take all the directions you give me."

He hummed to himself, clasping his hands in his lap. "I'll be paying you under the table, but as I told Gary, it will be generous. Just enough for you to get yourself that dress. But in exchange, I need your full attention this week. That means staying until the job is done. I requested my secretary not plan her wedding for this time of year, but clearly she did it anyway."

I giggled into my hand, sure he'd meant it as a joke, but his expression didn't change. I stopped and put it back in my lap.

He gestured behind me. "Grace left instructions at the desk for you. I'm not even sure what they are, but she should've outlined it all in the notes. You get one hour for lunch at noon, but other than that, you should be working on something at all times. If you need something to do, talk to June in reception. Try not to bother me unless it's absolutely pressing."

"Yes, sir," I said, standing. His eyes scanned over my eggshell blouse and grey slacks. The pants hung from my hips since the store had sold out of my size. I hadn't given it much thought at the time, but suddenly I wished I'd worn something a little more age appropriate.

"Where'd you get that outfit?" he asked.

"Um, Ann Taylor. I've never had an office job so I just—"

"No explanation necessary," he said, rising with me. "June takes lunch orders. You'll find my list of preferences in Grace's notes. If I'm feeling like something specific, I'll let you know. Otherwise choose from the list. You're dismissed."

I left the room with a dry throat. Walking into the office I'd felt apprehensive but easy. Suddenly my body was tight from his tone. His shift from my dad's friend to my boss was palpable, and I wasn't entirely sure who this man was. But I *was* sure of one thing—I did *not* want to piss him off.

CHAPTER 2

It was almost seven o'clock when I arrived at my empty dorm with Chinese takeout. My friends would've been in Cabo San Lucas for over forty-eight hours now and drunk more than half that time. I sighed, stripping off my bland button-down blouse and tossing it on the floor. I'd just changed into my pajamas when my cell phone rang with my dad's smiling picture.

"Hi, Dad."

"Hey, Sunshine. How'd it go today?"

I shrugged. "Fine. It was mostly boring, mindless projects. I never realized Dean was so uptight, though."

He chuckled lightly through the phone. "He takes business seriously. I doubt he's too keen about employing an eighteen-year-old for the week. If I were anyone else, he wouldn't have considered it."

"Why not?" I asked, my shoulders straightening. Dean had seemed more bothered by my outfit than my age.

"That position is for a woman whose career is being a secretary. Not a kid trying to save a few bucks between classes."

I sat at my desk, which doubled as a dining table, and picked at something invisible on its surface. "What could possibly be so hard about a secretarial job?"

"I wouldn't worry about it too much, Alex."

I pursed my lips. Mom and Dad expected me to go above and beyond in school and I'd always delivered. My first job shouldn't be any different.

"I'll give him a call," Dad continued. "See if I can't get him to ease up."

"No," I blurted. "It's fine. I just didn't know he was like that. I thought he was, like, cooler."

"Before his divorce, he was more devoted to that job than his own wife. After, he took it to an inhuman level. Everything he does is for that company. He makes time for me when I drive into L.A., but it's because I'm one of his only friends and I don't do it often."

I pulled at my bottom lip. Dean had still been at the office when he'd dismissed me for the night, and I'd only seen him leave long enough for a meeting partway through the day.

"But you're just a temp, Alex. I don't mind telling him to lighten up on you."

"No," I said, my mind made up. If Dean Brittany thought that job was too much for an eighteen-year-old, I'd prove him wrong—I'd be the best damn secretary that office had ever seen. "It's just a few days. I can take it."

"All right, then. Your call. Your mother says hello."

"Ask her why she sent me to Ann Taylor for work stuff. I'm the youngest one in the office by probably ten years, but I look the frumpiest."

"We've talked about this," Dad said in his attempt at a stern tone. "You need to cut back on the shopping. It's enough that we're paying all your expenses on top of your tuition. Don't you have a little money saved from your birthday? Maybe you can get a few outfits with that."

I glanced at the blouse on the floor, wondering why I cared when everyone I knew was gone the whole week. "Never mind," I said. "I'm there to save money, not spend it. I'll make it work."

"And, um—how are you, you know, *feeling*?"

I sighed. "Fine, I guess. Work is actually a good distraction. I only thought about Trey about a million times, which is an improvement."

"It'll get easier," he said. "I know sometimes a breakup can seem like the end of the world, but trust me, you'll get over it quicker than you think."

I shook my head. It didn't matter. Once Trey saw me in *the dress*, everything would change.

When I hung up the phone, I checked my texts, e-mails, and missed calls. Even though Trey was out of the country, I was tempted to send him a message. I'd hoped he'd have realized his mistake by now and called. I sniffled back the tears trying to break through, checking one last time to make sure I hadn't overlooked anything.

Fight it as I did, I couldn't help picturing him sprawled out under the Mexican sun with all our friends—tan, laughing, and chugging ice-cold Pacifico from the bottle. I should've been there too, but when he dumped me the week before we were supposed to leave, one of us had to stay behind.

The answer to getting him back was the dress. A few days earlier, during a well-deserved session of retail therapy, I'd locked myself in an oversized, white dressing room and stepped into gold. That's when I found the cure to my despair. The gilded sequins illuminated my tan, and my illuminated tan made me look thinner, fitter, and radiant. It hugged in all the right places. It was short without being indecent. It was a miracle dress. Against the sparkling metallic shine, my blonde hair was silky, smooth, and bright.

The night after I'd tried it on and been denied the money by my parents, Dad had mentioned Dean's temporary position. I knew then—the universe wanted me to have that dress. It wanted me to knock

Trey Richards off his feet so I could be there to help him back up.

CHAPTER 3

Tuesday morning, with my vow to impress my new boss fresh in my mind, I arrived at Brittany Industries twenty minutes early. Dean's closed door told me he was not to be disturbed—I knew this from a highlighted note left by Grace. I slunk into my office chair sheepishly, annoyed that his being early made me late.

My computer dinged with a message almost immediately.

Mr. Brittany
Welcome back, Ms. James.

I stared at the blinking box on Grace's computer. Did he think I wouldn't return?

Admin
Thank you. Can I get you coffee or anything?

Mr. Brittany
Got it already.

I read the message twice. Tomorrow I would just have to arrive early enough to have his coffee waiting for him. When he didn't continue, I picked up on Grace's list where I'd left off the night before.

Mr. Brittany
Which color is Ann Taylor today?

I blinked down to my blouse and touched the top button. That he'd noticed my outfit at all made me flush, but now I was sure he hadn't liked it.

Admin
Green.

Mr. Brittany
I suppose Grace failed to note that I'm extremely detail oriented.

Admin
She didn't. I'm sorry. It's light green. Not forest. Like gold-ish.

Mr. Brittany
So…pea-green.

I smiled to myself. That was exactly how I would've described it.

Admin
Yes. It's ugly.

He laughed from behind the closed door.

Mr. Brittany
I'll have the roast beef sandwich today.

Nothing came after that, so I opened Excel and began the tedious task of data entry. At some point I looked up to find June from reception hovering over my desk. Her pink blouse was far more fitted than mine, the button between her large breasts clinging for dear life.

"I need his lunch order," she said.

I glanced at the clock, surprised by the time. "The usual from around the corner."

"Cool. Some of us are going to O'Brady's in an hour. Want to come with?"

"I have plans," I said.

She shrugged. "Okay."

Just before noon, I knocked and entered Dean's office, unpacking food onto his desk and trying not to listen in on his conference call. Before I could leave the room, he called after me, covering the mouthpiece. "You're a Communications major, aren't you?"

I nodded.

"I need you to write me a press release before you leave tonight. My PR company is backed up, and it's too small to bother them with. Can you do that?"

"Yes," I said immediately. I'd never written one before but for some reason, I didn't want him to think I couldn't.

"You sure?" he asked with a hint of amusement.

I straightened my shoulders. "I can handle it."

"Then I'll e-mail the details. That's all."

I left the office shortly after, but it wasn't to eat. I drove to the closest mall, suddenly self-conscious about my wardrobe. I quickly picked some inexpensive things that were more similar to what the other girls wore. I hoped, as I looked at myself in the dressing room mirror, that Dean would like them.

* * * * *

It took me almost two hours to complete the press release. Each time Dean passed my desk, I shielded my computer screen with my body so he wouldn't see the several open windows explaining how to write one. He never looked, though. I waited until he was out of his office to place the finished product on his desk.

When he returned around four in the afternoon, I sat up and smiled, but he blew by me on his cell phone without even a nod. It was an hour before my computer pinged, drawing me from my work.

Mr. Brittany
Sheridan file

I had no idea what to make of it. I rifled through Grace's notes for a clue or hint as to who Sheridan was or to where files might be found. I left the desk. June was in the break room with a small group of girls from around the office.

"Um, June?" I started. "Mr. Brittany sent me a message that just said 'Sheridan file.'"

"I guess you figured out he's not a man of many words," June said.

I smiled. "He seems to speak a lot in commands."

The girls burst into laughter.

"What?" I asked.

"We have a running joke about what he'd be like in bed." She lengthened her spine in her chair and lowered her voice. "Touch my cock. Not like that. Lower. No. Higher."

Everyone giggled, but my throat felt thick.

"You look like you've seen a ghost," June teased me. "What's wrong?"

"I-I just—he's like fifty."

"So?" she asked. "He might be a little rigid but fifty or not, I'd fuck him."

I furrowed my brow as someone snickered. "What?"

"Have you seen the man?" asked a dark-haired girl. "He's sexier than most guys I've met my own age."

"He's definitely handsome, but…" I paused. He *was* attractive. On my way into work, I'd attributed the flutter in my stomach to nerves, but maybe it'd been more than that. "He's, like, my dad's friend. Do people his age even have sex anymore?"

The room was silent a moment. Then there was more laughter, even louder this time.

"How old are you?" someone asked.

"Eighteen."

"Oh, sweetie. You have a lot to learn still."

I cringed. "But my dad uses Viagra."

June snickered as she said, "So then obviously your dad still *does it.*"

"Gross." I shook my head. "I can't think about that. Do you know what that Sheridan message meant?"

She nodded and stood to lead me to the filing room. I located the one marked "Sheridan" quickly since they were alphabetized and hurried back to his office. I knocked once and entered. "I have the file, Mr. Brittany," I said.

"Great," he muttered without looking up.

I set it down and furtively scanned his desk for the press release.

"Was there something else?" he asked and glanced up. His eyes stopped on my new pencil skirt only long enough for me to notice. It sat high on my waist, hugging every slight curve on the way down. This time it was my size, maybe even a little small. I'd paired it with a fitted, heather grey "V" neck sweater that stopped at the very top of my cleavage.

"Did you change?" he asked.

"I spilled coffee on my *green* blouse, so I ran out at lunch."

His eyes flickered over my face until the silence became uncomfortable.

"Wait," he said as I turned to leave. "Alexandra?"

I looked back. "Yes?"

He flipped through a stack of papers on his desk and held up the release. "What is this?" he asked.

"Um, the press release you asked for earlier. Was something wrong?"

"Yes," he answered. "Three somethings."

I bit my bottom lip hard. That couldn't be possible. I'd checked it over and over for any possible mistakes. "I'm sorry."

"In the future, don't bring me anything that's not perfect." He showed me the paper again before placing it flat on the desk. He nodded at it, beckoning me. I walked to the edge.

"See this?" he asked. With a red pen, he made a circle on the page.

I leaned in. "Um."

"Come closer."

I bent forward, twisting my head to see where he was pointing.

"Closer."

I glanced up. For the first time since he'd shifted into boss mode, his deep blue eyes sparked. He nodded me on with an expectant look, so I folded myself over the desk. He held up his palm, stopping me at a ninety-degree angle.

"Comfortable?" he asked.

"Not really," I said tentatively.

"Then rest your elbows."

My eyes widened. It was an unnatural position, one that didn't seem appropriate for the workplace. I I held his gaze and placed my forearms on the desk's surface. He looked at my hands, balled into fists. When he didn't speak, I uncurled all my fingers and flattened them so they framed the release.

"Here," he said, indicating a sentence, "the verbiage is entirely wrong."

I swallowed dryly. "I'm sorry. I'm not that familiar with your industry."

"Is that an excuse?"

"No. I'll fix it."

"The whole thing is too long. I need you to cut it to about half but keep the same amount of information."

My breasts were directly in his line of vision, baring my cleavage to him. They rose and fell faster with the increase of my heart rate, but he didn't look once. His eyes only jumped between my face and the desk.

"Yes, sir."

"And here," he said, tapping the end of his pen on the paper, "you forgot a comma."

"I'll fix that too."

He handed it to me. "Get it to me before you leave. You're dismissed."

I'd done something wrong, but it wasn't just my errors. A pit formed in my stomach when I thought of my breasts in his face. Yet he hadn't even looked.

It took me over an hour to correct my mistakes because the release was already as concise as I'd thought possible. This time, I e-mailed it to avoid disturbing him.

He stayed locked in his office until well after six. I stayed too. There was plenty to do since I'd barely made it past the second page of Grace's list. Every few minutes as I worked on a task, my mind would float back to me in that position, and how he'd commanded me there. Had it been harmless? Was I making something of nothing?

Right before seven o'clock, a message from Dean popped up on my screen.

Mr. Brittany
Open the door.

I rose slowly and brushed an invisible wrinkle from my skirt. I'd assumed he'd forgotten about me and wouldn't realize it until his way out of the office. I turned and walked to open his door. Reclined in his leather chair with the phone to his ear, he didn't look up. His tone was deep with authority as he spoke into the receiver. Since he gave me no further instructions, I returned to my desk. The back of my neck tingled as I imagined him watching me from his seat. That feeling remained until I received another message.

Mr. Brittany
You forgot the comma.

My heart skipped. I'd forgotten a comma? On the press release? But I'd been careful, making sure the release was just the right length, and—my fingers curled into fists. He was right. I'd been so concerned about the length, I'd forgotten to go back and add the comma. I unleashed a string of curses in my head as I stared at the screen, no idea how to proceed. I could still hear him on the phone, his words calm while my heart raced.

Mr. Brittany
Come in here so I can show you.

He'd shown me earlier. I didn't need to see it again. But I silenced my nerves, stood up and entered the office. When I passed through the doorway, he glanced up. His eyes were heavy, staring at me as though he'd never stop. Like there was nothing else in the world to look at. Something about his expression slowed my steps. It was a few stretched moments until I reached him. I stood in that spot, waiting. He pulled out the press release from his pile.

"Give it until tomorrow," he said into the phone with his eyes still on me. "If it's the same, place the order." He nodded at the paper. I looked between it and his face. Finally, I bent over, resuming my earlier position.

"And if it drops lower, buy double." He hung up the phone without another word and looked at me. "Remember what I said earlier, Alexandra?"

"Don't bring it to you until it's perfect."

"Is this perfect?"

"No," I said softly.

"How do you suggest I handle this?"

He stood suddenly, and my heart jumped against my ribcage.

"Are you going to fire me?" I asked, my voice small.

He chuckled and came around to my side of the desk. "That's a little extreme, don't you think?"

"I-I don't know."

"And I don't think your dad would appreciate it. What are some other ways we can ensure this doesn't happen again?"

I went to straighten up and face him, but his hand touched my shoulder, keeping me there. With another step, his hips were within inches of mine.

"Um…" I couldn't see his face—it was unnerving. My entire body tensed, alert as if danger were near. My mind searched for a response. I'd been careless. I would've been upset if I weren't so thrown off by my position. And, in a way, I was more curious about how he'd *handle* this. "You could punish me," I said. "Take away my lunch break?"

"I'm not sure that's incentive enough. I could take away your chair so you have to stand all day."

There had to be laws against that. It seemed ridiculously unjust for a measly little comma. Only, I knew it wasn't about the comma. It was deeper than that. It was about my inattention to detail, when details meant everything to Dean. The punishment had to be a grand gesture on my part to show him I understood. Forfeiting my pay for the day? Offering to work a weekend? My eyes focused on the spot where the comma should be. "I'll do whatever you need me to," I said. "I'll even—"

A hard sting landed against my backside. I cried out in surprise. What was happening? Had he just *spanked* me? With his hand? "Dean," I rushed out, my mind spinning faster than I could keep up. "What—"

"Mr. Brittany," he corrected calmly and delivered another slap.

I had to leave. His hand secured me against the desk, even as I tried to stand. He spanked me a third time, the smack resounding between my legs.

"That one was for squirming," he said. "Now, fix the comma, e-mail it to me, and you can go home."

I remained glued to the desk in stunned silence. It was as though he expected me to act as if nothing had happened. I couldn't. I was enraged. You couldn't spank a grown adult—and certainly not one who worked for you. My impulse to flee had passed, and now I was seemingly immobile. My throat closed as I urged myself to speak up, to put him in his place, to run through the office screaming about what had just been done to me. My ass smarted, just enough to keep his commands fresh. I finally found it in myself to get into an upright position. Instead of all those things I wanted to do, I kept my eyes on the floor and hurried back to my desk.

My eyes blurred with tears as I fixed the document. It hadn't particularly hurt, though. It'd sent something up my spine—almost like a thrill. His firm touch lingered on my shoulder. Shock and embarrassment were red-hot on my ass. I almost wanted to feel that slap again, but more than that, I wanted to race home and tell my dad everything so he could handle this. Perhaps with a lawsuit or public shaming to all of their mutual friends. The press might even be interested in hearing about the kinky bastard behind Brittany Industries. Certainly I wasn't returning to that office again—ever.

Back in my dorm, I found my cell phone in my purse and dialed my dad immediately.

"Hi, Sunshine," he said. "How was work?"

"It was—you wouldn't *believe...*"

"That bad, huh? Dean hasn't eased up at all?"

Silence descended on the line as I grasped for a response. How could I tell Dad his precious Sunshine had just been spanked by his best friend? And for something so ridiculous? "Um, not really."

"Let me talk to him."

I squeezed my eyes shut and played that conversation in my head. My ass throbbed at the memory of Dean's office. I squirmed in my chair. And...there was my beautiful gold dress. "It's okay," I said, surprising myself. "It's only a week. I'll take care of it myself."

"Proud of you," he said. There was a smile in his voice. "You've got this."

I went to bed early, still unsure of how to handle the situation. What Dean had done was so basely wrong that I couldn't help wondering what made him believe he'd get away with it. I touched my backside. Any indication of my punishment was completely gone. Was it a one-time thing? Did he treat his other employees that way? I pictured June in my position on the desk, her large breasts squished against the surface. I frowned. Maybe he hadn't looked at my breasts because June was his type. She was older, more mature, and I doubted she ever wore pea-green.

I was just his friend's kid, pretending to be an adult for a week.

It wasn't until I was drifting asleep that I realized I hadn't thought of Trey in hours.

CHAPTER 4

In the elevator, I squared my shoulders and tugged on the hem of my new navy blazer. I had no idea what I'd say to Dean, but I couldn't just let this go. Today he would be embarrassed and apologize. Once he'd taken the night to consider what a sexual harassment suit could do to his company, he might even grovel. The question was whether I'd forgive him and let it go.

As soon as I'd set my purse down, he called for me from behind his closed door. I entered without knocking, and when he looked up, my eyes narrowed. Instead of shame, amusement etched his features. His cocky half-smile was a slap in the face, but unexpectedly, it also made my cheeks hot. His smirk was... what?

June's crass declaration came to mind. *"I'd fuck him."*

His smirk was somehow *sexy*.

"I expected a call from your dad last night," he said.

I shook my head. "I didn't tell him."

"And you returned."

"Only to tell you how wrong—how *terrible* it was." I took a step farther into the office and raised my chin. "You shouldn't have done that."

"You're right. I shouldn't have."

"Because that's completely inappropriate for the workplace."

"Then you'd be okay with it outside the office?"

"What? No," I snapped, flushing even redder. "That's not what I meant. Why would I want you to–to do *that* to me? Ever?"

His face twisted as he tried unsuccessfully to suppress a grin. "Come over here."

"Absolutely not."

"Are you leaving?"

"Leaving?" I repeated. "I don't know. I haven't decided."

"So until you decide, you still work for me?"

I glanced at his hand resting on the arm of his chair and then back at his eyes. "I guess."

"Then," he said, pausing before delivering his words slowly, "get over here."

My fingers twisted in front of me. No dress was worth this humiliation. But I wanted to feel that sting again. I craved it. It was the first thing I'd thought of when I'd woken up. My feet disobeyed me, walking around the desk, stopping beside his chair. He stood in one fluid motion, dwarfing me instantly and drawing my eyes upward.

"I couldn't help but notice you're wearing the same skirt."

"I don't have much to choose from," I said. "I wasn't going to blow all my money on a new wardrobe for one week."

"I'm not complaining. It's better than those hideous pants you wore yesterday before the coffee got to them."

He said *coffee* as though he knew I'd been lying. It didn't matter—I wasn't the guilty one here. My jaw set. "You can't speak to me that way."

"By the way, I'm forty-eight," he said with raised eyebrows.

"What?"

"Not fifty."

Embarrassment burnt a quick course through my body as I realized he'd overheard my conversation in the break room. We'd all giggled, but Dean didn't look the least bit amused. My face was on fire.

"You think people my age don't fuck?" he asked.

I gasped, almost choking at the word.

He grabbed my hand roughly and brought it to the front of his pants. My palm pressed into the solid hardness that strained against his zipper.

"We do," he said. "Is that enough evidence for you, Alexandra?"

My mouth opened and closed, my hand trembled. He slid it up so I felt the ridges of his crown through the fabric.

"I'm not…I can't do this."

"You don't have to do anything," he said. His smile was too easy. When he released me, my skin was suddenly ice cold. He'd been warm, substantial in my hand. He seemed twice the size of Trey, and even more so since he towered over me.

"Does Grace do this for you?" I whispered.

He threw his head back and laughed. "No. Nobody does anything for me, Alex. I have a strict rule against office relations."

"Oh."

"I spanked you last night because I wanted to. Because it made me horny as hell. It took everything I had not to tear off that tight skirt and take you right there."

My mouth was hanging open, but I couldn't seem to close it. I glanced down at the skirt and back up. My brain struggled, and all I could think was that it'd taken Trey close to two months to ask me out, and another couple weeks to make a move.

"Fortunately," Dean said, "in the nick of time, I remembered the many reasons that could never happen."

I snapped my jaw shut. *Never.* The way he said it was so final, so curt, the way he normally was. My gaze fell from his eyes to his lips. The word *sexy* sizzled in my mind, and I realized it had been since June had said it in the break room. "Because of your office policy?" I asked.

"You're off limits. Aside from the fact that you work for me, your father's my good friend. And even if he weren't, you're just a girl."

"A girl?" I gaped. I was an adult. I wore business attire. The thought quickly faded when I realized something else. "You would—you *want* that? With me?"

He blinked slowly as a lazy smile formed on his face. It was disarming when his normally stoic expression broke. "Do I want that? With you? It doesn't matter if I do. I can't touch you."

"You just did."

"Only to prove a point. I can't have you out there spreading rumors that I can't get it up."

I knew I should go. I wasn't even sure why I'd gotten dressed for work at all, when all I'd meant to do was come in and quit.

"Go back to work," he said. "I won't bother you again."

Back to work. For him. Right outside his office. Where he could call me in at any time. "So if I stay— you don't expect me to…"

"No. But you're a beautiful girl, Alexandra. I can't promise I won't fantasize about you. Sometimes," he said, "when you're right in front of me."

29

His words delivered a sharp but warm tingle deep in my stomach. He licked his lips briefly. He was thinking of me now. How? Bent over his desk? In his fantasy, did it go further than that?

"If that doesn't bother you, stay the rest of the week. If it does…" He paused, gesturing to the door. "I'll still give you your money so you can get your dress."

"I don't need your money," I said quickly, backing away.

"You're smarter than that," he said, his eyes twinkling. "Take the money. But this is the only time I'll offer it. If you don't leave now, then you have to finish out the week. Otherwise I won't pay you a dime."

I had more respect than that. Even though part of me wanted to stay, I wasn't sure how I possibly could. "I'll clear out my desk."

A deep chuckle was all I heard as I turned my back. On the other side of the door, I sat and stared at nothing. There was no anger bubbling inside me even though I thought there should be. There was only confusion.

I wasn't ready to say goodbye to Dean. He'd always been intriguing. And yes—*sexy*. How hadn't I seen it before?

But how could I stay? I put my head in my hands, and my elbow nudged the mouse. The computer screen came to life. Microsoft Outlook brimmed with unread e-mails. Checking over my shoulder once, I quickly opened the top one and responded before moving to the next one.

I didn't stop until the door squeaked open behind me. "You're still here."

I squinted at the time. It'd been two hours since I'd declared I was leaving.

"It's only for the week," Dean said. I looked up at him. "And it's already Wednesday. If you want to stay, stay. Don't overthink it. Either way, Chinese for lunch. If you're leaving, tell June on your way out."

He shut the door, and I returned my eyes to the computer screen. I told myself I was going. I even packed up my purse and set it on the desk. But Dean's hand slapping against my ass made something bloom between my legs. And his dick—it was nothing like Trey's. I could still feel it, hard, thick, hot against my palm. He'd said he'd keep his hands to himself. Just a fantasy—*me*, as someone else's fantasy. I put my purse back under my desk.

Trey's face when he saw me in my gold dress would be worth everything. I'd never accept Dean's money without doing the work, so I made the decision to stay. Things were already uncomfortable—how much worse could they get?

31

CHAPTER 5

It wasn't until five o'clock on the dot that I heard anything from Dean again. That didn't mean I hadn't been thinking of him though, just inside that office, possibly thinking of me too. There was no ridding myself of him when he was that close. He was a force, radiating even from behind the closed door. He was taking hold of me, and it seemed to be growing stronger by the hour.

Mr. Brittany
I need you to stay late. Cancel your plans.

Admin
I had no plans.

Mr. Brittany

Even better. Open the door. I like to watch you work.

I hesitated. My chance to take a stand and leave had passed, though. I'd given him permission to fantasize about me. To watch me. My inner thighs sweat as I pressed them together unnaturally hard. To keep him out? To imagine him there when I thought of him? I wasn't sure.

I opened the door, but he was so focused on his computer that he didn't seem to notice. I took my seat again, brushing my long hair over my shoulders. My back was straighter than ever. I continued working, but with each tap of my fingers against the keyboard, my thoughts grew louder. I sensed his eyes on me. Or, I wanted them there. Watching. Imagining. Feeling me without touching. I swallowed dryly, warm in a way I wasn't used to. I was glad for the distraction when he forwarded me instructions on an urgent project. After forty minutes, his name appeared on the screen.

Mr. Brittany
Blackthorne file

The office was dark and empty except for our corner. The file room buzzed to life when I switched on its fluorescent lights. I pulled open the heavy drawer marked "A, B, C" and fingered through it. On my way back, I tripped over a snag in the carpet and papers flew out of the file in my hand.

I cursed under my breath, getting on my knees to gather up the mess.

As I grasped the last sheet, Dean's voice came from the office through the open door. "Bring me the file."

"That's what I'm doing," I said.

"Just like that."

I glanced up and met his eyes, darkened into an unnatural indigo. "What?"

"Bring it to me on your knees."

My mind chose that moment to conjure up the image of my friends, probably basking in Mexico's hot sun, flirting with people their age and sipping Piña Coladas. Would they laugh if they saw me now? Tease me? I didn't think it was so funny. In fact, my thighs trembled under Dean's—no, *Mr. Brittany's*—unrelenting gaze.

I clutched the file in my hand.

"Put it down your skirt," he said.

I tucked it into my waistband and waited.

"Now," he said, "just crawl."

I fell forward onto my hands. My palms and knees scratched against the carpet as I went to him. I crept slowly, drawn in by his beckoning eyes. The papers crinkled against my stomach, the file folder's edges poking into my blouse.

"When I get home, I'm going to think of you this way," he said evenly, talking to my breasts, which swung in my button-down as I advanced. "Except, in my fantasy, I'd get up and walk over to you. I'd pull up your skirt and take you from behind."

I stopped in my tracks. I wanted to tell him he could, but my mouth felt dry, my heart sped. He didn't give me the chance anyway.

"When I was close, I'd pull out and come all over your ass."

I inhaled sharply.

"Has anybody ever come on you before, Alexandra?"

I shook my head and continued across the floor, closing in on his desk.

"Are you a virgin?"

"No," I whispered.

"Do you want me to?"

"Want you to what?" I asked.

"Come on you."

My chest vibrated now with the force of my heartbeat. I shook my head, because I couldn't think of anything more degrading. I wouldn't even let Trey ejaculate in my mouth. When I reached Dean, I remained on my hands and knees, waiting.

"Do you have a boyfriend?"

My eyes fell to his pant leg. "He dumped me."

"Look at me." He sat back in his chair, assessing me. "How come?"

"He said he didn't want a girlfriend anymore."

"I thought you wanted the dress for the formal."

"His frat brother is taking me as a favor. The dress is…"

"Is this frat brother trying to screw you?"

"No," I exclaimed. "It's just so Trey will see me at the formal and want me back."

"Have you slept with anyone else?"

"Just Trey."

"Did you suck him off?"

"Yes."

"Are you good at it?"

My eyelashes fluttered, and I shifted on my knees. "I'm not sure."

"Am I making you uncomfortable?"

"Yes."

"How come?"

"*The Little Mermaid.*"

"I'm sorry?"

"You took Vivian and me once. To see it. They had a special matinee viewing in the theater when we were younger."

"I remember. And that makes you uncomfortable because now I want to fuck you."

My heart leaped into my throat as I stared at him.

"That's right. I want to bury myself in your sweet, eighteen-year-old pussy. I haven't been able to think of anything else all day." He glanced behind me. My hips were wiggling. "Does that turn you on?"

My entire body thrummed. The thought of that large thing I'd held earlier near me, inside me—it was all I could think about. "Yes," I admitted.

"If you have any doubt about a man my age, I'll tell you this—anything you let that boy do to you, I've already perfected."

Sex with Trey had been fine, but Dean made it sound like something else entirely. What did it mean that he'd perfected it? I wanted to know. I needed it. A rush of warmth made my body seem heavy. I was still on my hands and knees, poised, my lips parted as I stared up at him.

"Don't look at me like that," he said. "I'm not going to touch you. Just know I'll be thinking of you in this exact position when I jerk off later."

The idea of that weighty cock in his hand almost bowled me over. I might've fallen at his feet if not for his next command.

"Give me the file."

I sat back on my calves and slipped the papers from my waistband.

"Alexandra?"

"Yes?"

"Since I can't touch you, tell me one thing."

"Okay."

"How does it feel?"

My brows gathered. "What?"

"Just put your hand between your legs, and tell me how it feels."

I gulped through my panic. Could I do this? Was I sure the office was empty—and why was that my main concern? I spread my knees wider. He was patient, watching until I bunched up my skirt just enough to slip my hand under. I was sensitive, slightly swollen with arousal. "It feels…all right."

"No. I mean, tell me how your panties feel."

"They're soft."

"What else?"

"A little…damp, I guess."

"Christ. What color?"

I searched my memory. "Pink. It's a thong from Victoria's Secret."

"How do *you* feel? Inside of them?"

I swallowed. No way I would touch myself here in this office. I already felt weird with my hand under my skirt. I shifted them aside fractionally. My body wanted more, but I ignored it and ran a gentle finger over myself. "Also soft and damp," I said quietly. "And also…pink."

"Fuck." He grunted and put his hand over the crotch of his pants. "That's enough. You're dismissed."

I remained still, trying not to look at the bulge under his palm. He wanted me to leave *now*? I was hot. Bothered. Unhinged. Almost enough to ask *him* to touch me. "Dismissed? But—"

"Go."

Before I even stood, he'd returned his attention to his computer. I didn't know how he could be so casual when in my eyes, the earth had just tilted on its axis. My entire body felt like an exposed nerve aching for his soothing touch. My heart pounded all the way down the elevator. I slid into the front seat of my car, unable to think of anything other than Mr. Brittany taking me from behind.

CHAPTER 6

I arrived an hour early the next day, and by the time Dean strode off the elevator, I had hot coffee waiting on his desk. I smiled, but his answering nod was short.

The next few hours, I glanced up every time he passed my desk, but he never returned my look. By early evening, I was beginning to wonder if I'd imagined it all or if I'd done something wrong—or even something to lose his interest.

For me, it was the opposite. It was as if he'd flipped me on like a light switch but forgotten to turn me off. Finally, I got the message I hadn't realized I'd been desperately hoping for.

Mr. Brittany
Do you have your cell on you?

Admin
Yes.

Mr. Brittany
Go to the bathroom. Finger yourself. Record it. Bring it to me. No less than two fingers.

I blinked repeatedly at the screen. Was he serious? I'd never let anyone watch me touch myself before. I was at work. I glanced around the office. From my vantage point, I couldn't see anyone in the next room. There was only the melodic, ubiquitous tap of fingertips against keyboards.

Mr. Brittany
Hurry. I'm especially impatient today.

I got up quickly from my desk and grabbed my purse. I had no idea how he knew I was still sitting there since the door was closed. I made my way to the bathroom, unable to believe I was going to do this. Inside, I locked myself into a stall and hung my purse on the hook. I waited a moment, listening for anyone even though the bathroom was empty. I pulled up my new dress. My grey slacks were still a crumpled pile in my car from Tuesday.

I located my cell and set it up to record. Awkwardly, I held it just near my underwear and let my other hand explore. I hooked my fingers into my

42

thong and pulled it down around my thighs. I teased myself, and when I was warm and wet, slipped a finger inside. Remembering his message, I immediately added another finger. I bit my lip to keep from making any noise.

When the door opened, I froze, two fingers deep inside myself and everything tight and aching. I almost told them to get out, wanting nothing more than to chase my orgasm. To keep it from slipping away, I squeezed my eyes shut and imagined Dean spanking me over his desk, fully clothed as he made me stare at the paper's red marks. As soon as I was alone again, I plunged my fingers deeper—searching, massaging, until I came. My heavy breathing was the only sound echoing in the bathroom. I hit the stop button and fixed my dress before returning to my desk.

"Come in," he said when I knocked.

I entered the office. For the first time, he turned his body from the computer and gave me his full attention. "Did you do what I asked?"

"Yes," I said, showing him the cell phone.

He glanced at it and back at me. "Two fingers?"

"Yes."

"I was right about you. You do follow direction well." He nodded his head once so I walked toward him. "God, how I'd like to taste you," he said.

"Taste me?" I asked, confused. "Like, kiss me?"

"No." I followed his eyes and realized he'd been looking at my hand, not my cell. He took the phone from me, but my hand remained suspended in the air. I opened it for him. I couldn't believe what I was offering, but that didn't stop me. He shook his head. "No touching. Do it for me."

I crinkled my nose. "I don't know…"

His expression remained as stern as his back was straight. After a moment I touched the pad of my finger to the tip of my tongue.

"Both," he said in an unusually soft voice.

I put the fingers I'd used to masturbate in my mouth and sucked. He looked momentarily gone, but then I lost his attention to the video. He watched it intently, his eyes narrowing, his head cocking.

"Don't you shave?"

"No," I said. Trey had teased me about the fact that I would only trim. It was what I liked, though, so that was how I'd always kept it. Now I wished I'd listened to him and shaved everything off or even waxed—anything to show Dean I could be like the sophisticated women he knew.

"It's perfect," he said.

"It is?"

He looked back at my face and set the phone down, even though the video wasn't over. He assessed me, almost as if seeing me for the first time. My soft moans from the cell phone surrounded us as we stared at each other. They grew louder, more insistent. I didn't remember moaning that way, and as they filled the office, my core grew hotter with the throbbing between my legs.

"I thought about you," I said, my voice unintentionally husky.

"I know."

I bunched the fabric of my skirt in two fists. "I think I might...want this."

"I know that too."

"How? How do you know?"

He stood slowly, speaking, but I barely heard a thing. My ears were loud with the rush of arousal in my system. His jaw flexed while his nostrils flared.

"What?" I asked.

"I said, 'Have a nice evening.'"

"Evening?" I repeated. "I didn't finish my project."

"You can finish it tomorrow."

His face was stoic, but I caught the surprise in his eyes when I stepped closer. "I thought it was urgent."

"It is urgent. But I have an event tonight, and I'm late to pick up my date."

I instantly took a step back. "What?"

"For the third time, have a nice evening," he said, turning away. "I'll see you in the morning."

I snatched my phone from his desk. "I'm taking my video with me."

"That's fine." He pulled open the door to what looked like a closet. "I'm finished with it."

I had no choice but to leave, and I scowled as I did.

CHAPTER 7

Dean cleared his throat, and my head snapped up.

"You're here early," he said, glancing at his watch.

"My special project pushed back the rest of my to-do list. Since it's my last day, I figured I'd better get an early start."

He raised an eyebrow, pleased. "You really want that dress, don't you?"

I looked away.

"That's not it," he said thoughtfully. "All this for a boy." He leaned in when my eyes drifted up to his again. "To let you go, this boy must not be very smart. And frankly, I don't like the idea of you dating someone who's not very smart."

A smile tugged at the corners of my lips. "Thank you, Mr. Brittany."

"On the bright side, you only have to call me that until tonight," he said.

He walked past me into his office, and my smile fell a little. His cologne lingered for minutes after he'd left. I pulled out my cell phone and swiped through some photos of my short relationship with Trey. I stopped on one of us at Lake Havasu, me in my bikini, waving my beer at the camera. Trey was shirtless, smiling big, his baseball cap backwards. I glanced behind me at Dean's closed door. They were certainly different. Dean seemed to be twice Trey's size. *That's because he's here, now, in front of me.* I shook my head and put the phone away.

By noon I was putting the finishing touches on some basic website copy. I checked it for the third time, pleased with the final product. As I went to send it, I paused. It was my last day. My last chance to feel Dean next to me. I reopened Word, chewing on the inside of my bottom lip. If I could get in his office and close the door, I'd feel better. Satisfied. Even if nothing could happen. I deleted a comma. Before I lost my nerve, I reattached the document and mailed it. I let out the breath I'd been holding.

After twenty minutes, he called for me. "Alexandra? Can I see you?"

I stood and entered his office, closing the door behind me.

"I didn't tell you to shut the door." He leaned back in his large chair and spoke again before I could make any move. "You seem to have some trouble with comma usage."

"Oh. I'm sorry, Mr. Brittany."

"How sorry?"

"Very sorry. It was careless."

"Indeed it was. I've run out of ideas to demonstrate how I feel about mistakes."

I wrung my fingers together. "You could...do what you did before?"

"Except, it doesn't seem that was very effective."

I nodded earnestly. "It was."

"There's also the issue of no touching."

I stepped forward hesitantly. When he didn't stop me, I continued up to the desk, bending over it with my elbows in position. "You don't have to touch me to spank me," I said.

His eyes fell to my cleavage. Without removing them, he reached out to open his top desk drawer. "What a little devil you've become," he murmured as he rummaged through the drawer's contents. When he found what he was looking for, he stood. There was a slapping noise, and I turned my head. His hand curled around a wooden ruler as he tapped it against his open palm. He came so close, I could only feel his body heat. As he raised the ruler, I said, "Wait."

"It's too late for wait," he said.

I reached back and lifted my skirt over my ass, pulling it around my waist.

I could hear his inhale behind me. "Alex—"

"Now I'm ready."

It wasn't a second before the ruler stung my backside. I moaned, my fingernails curling into my palms.

I started when the ruler landed a second time. "What was that one for?" I asked.

"For telling me to wait." The wood came down hard against my ass cheek again. "And that's for talking back."

I spread my legs slightly to ease the pain, and he smacked me once more. "That's for teasing me. I don't do teasing, Alexandra. I'm used to getting exactly what I want."

I turned my head over my shoulder and bit my lip. "Are you saying you want me?"

"Like you wouldn't believe."

"It's a shame you can't have me then." I slid down the desk, away from him. He took a step, but I shook my head. "No, Mr. Brittany."

"You're telling me no?"

I nodded. "No touching."

I rested my cheek against the wood desk and blinked up at him. His eyes shifted when I lowered my hand between my legs.

"Alexandra…"

I moved my thong aside. "It really *is* a shame," I said. "Because just the thought is—it's making me…"

"Wet?" he finished.

"I want you too."

"You do?"

I lifted my head because he sounded surprised. Wasn't it obvious? Couldn't he feel the way my desire had begun to take over everything the last couple days? My heart pounded. I was suddenly nervous about saying it aloud. "I-I…well, I thought—"

He stepped around me and leaned forward, placing his hands on both sides of my head. He still didn't touch me. "This week has been torture," he said.

I clenched my teeth. "Nobody has to know."

"I can't. It's wrong."

Before he could say another word, I began rubbing myself underneath him. I moaned against the desk. "I want you," I said. "I want it to be your fingers."

He lowered his mouth to my ear. "Do you know how sexy you are? Touching yourself like this?"

"If I were yours—"

"If you were mine, I'd drop on my knees right now and eat your pussy like it was my last meal."

I gasped. His words alone had me thrusting my hips against my own palm.

"That's good, Alexandra. I want to watch you come. Can you picture me fucking you right now?"

"Yes," I said.

I froze at a knock on the door.

"Don't stop," he said. "Whatever you do, don't stop."

His heat lit up my skin. His voice echoed in my ears, the deepest thing I'd ever heard.

"What is it?" he called out.

June's voice came from behind the door. "Where's Alex? She's not supposed to leave your desk. Your phone's been ringing."

"I sent her on an errand," he snapped. "Just take messages for her."

My other hand shot out and gripped the opposite lip of the desk. I pulled myself harder against my hand.

"Fuck," he whispered. I could sense him just behind my ass, and I wanted nothing more than to push back against him. So I did.

He groaned, grabbed my hips roughly, pulled me back into him again and then let go like I was on fire.

"Dean," I begged.

"I told you I'd fantasize about you. Right before I promised you—and myself—that I wouldn't touch you."

"I need it. I've never felt this…this—"

"Goddamn it." Metal clinked. He was undoing his belt. "Hold on to that desk, Alexandra. You're about to get fucked."

He pushed my hand aside and plunged a finger in me as me as I cried out. His zipper hissed, and he fingered me harder. I latched both hands onto the edge of the desk so I was stretched across it. "Oh, God. Dean."

His fingers withdrew, and he slapped my ass cheek.

"M-Mr. Brittany," I corrected.

The head of his cock pressed against my opening. I wanted to look, to watch his domination of my body, but he placed a hand in the center of my back and pinned me down.

"I tried, Alex, I did. But you love to tease me, don't you?"

"No," I whimpered.

One strong thrust filled me with his cock and jolted me into the desk. His hand dug into my back, holding me in place as his hips drew back and collided into me again. Within seconds he was fucking me fast and rough, completely different than Trey ever had. There was confidence in his every move, as if he knew I wouldn't break no matter how hard he gave it to me.

He closed over my back, his breath hot near my ear. One of his hands gripped the desk right next to mine and his other moved my hair.

"So I can watch your face as you come," he said, pounding me. "The way you're biting your lip, squeezing your eyes shut, gasping harder the deeper I go—God, you're fucking sexy."

My knuckles whitened.

"Come," he said.

My teeth were dangerously close to breaking the skin of my lip. I was close, almost there, but I couldn't seem to catch my orgasm.

His heat left my back as he smacked me twice as hard as earlier. "I said *come*, Alexandra."

The burn of his slap spread like wildfire throughout me. I convulsed, coming with a fervor I'd never experienced. Even after I'd finished, my body quaked with aftershocks.

He pulled out suddenly, but I lay deflated against the desk.

"Get up," he said.

My arms were shaky as I hoisted myself up. He walked around the desk and sat in his leather chair.

"Come over here."

I followed. His pants were barely undone so just his cock, wet from my pussy, was visible. "On your knees and suck," he said.

I blinked, but my body seemed to be in his command, not mine. I felt small and uncertain at his feet, having only ever blown Trey—and I could see now that this was entirely different. I tested him by licking just the crown, and he groaned up at the ceiling. One of his hands curled around the arm of his chair. His other hand threaded in my hair and pulled. I closed my lips over him and took him to the back of my throat, but I still couldn't reach the base. My hand wrapped around him, my tongue making its way up and down his shaft.

The phone buzzed somewhere in the background.

"Mr. Brittany?" June said through the speakerphone.

My head snapped up when he answered, "Yes?"

I gasped, and he shushed me silently.

"I have a Mr. James on the line for you."

My eyes widened so fast, I thought they'd pop out of their sockets.

Dean smiled slowly, his eyes amused. "Alexandra's dad? Put him through."

"Dean—!"

He grabbed his cock and pushed it against my lips. I opened my mouth instinctively, and his other hand urged my head down.

"Gary," Dean said coolly. "To what do I owe the—*pleasure*?"

"Hey, Dean. Just calling to thank you for helping us out with Alexandra this week. I know you've been giving it to her tough, but I think it's been good for her."

Dean's hand in my hair controlled my head, gently but firmly. My mouth glided over his hardness, and I could already feel myself getting wet again.

"I must say I'm impressed with your daughter," Dean said. "She's much more driven than I realized. Hardworking too. Not one job I gave her went unfinished."

I glanced up at him from under my lashes, and he winked. I moved my hand up and down faster with the same rhythm that my head bobbed.

"F—I have to go, Gary. I'll—"

"Sure, sure. I know you're busy. Did Alex take a late lunch or something? Why didn't she answer your phone?"

"Yes. She's eating. Got her mouth full at the moment, actually."

I heard the phone beep as he hung up the call, and I pulled my head up, gasping. "Dean! What—"

"Keep going, Alexandra, please," he said with a hint of pleading. I'd never seen any man look that way, least of all him. I would've done anything for that powerless look on Dean, who never let his control slip. I took his cock again, sucking hard and pumping my fist at the same time. Before long, he came, gripping my hair so I couldn't pull away.

"Christ," he said, his chest heaving, and his shoulders slumping against the chair.

I coughed, wiping him from my lips.

"Sorry," he said with a smile that bordered on smirking. "Guess I should've warned you first."

"You came in my mouth!"

He laughed. "Don't tell me you're a spitter."

I frowned, sitting back on my calves.

Dean shook his head. "That wasn't your first blowjob was it?"

"No," I snapped. "I told you already. I just never let him—*you know*—in my mouth. Even though he begged."

"He sounds like a pussy."

This time I smirked. "Asshole is more like it."

He caught my chin with his hand. "Pretty little thing," he said, "but what a dirty mouth."

I stared up at him, and his eyes held mine, just like his hand held my face. There was a tense moment, as though he wanted to say something, but he let me go instead. "You should probably go clean up."

I nodded and got to my feet.

"Almost made it the whole week," he muttered, "but you're damned impossible to resist."

I blushed and fixed my clothing, running a hand through my hair before I left for the bathroom. Even though I hadn't brought anything with me into his office, I couldn't help feeling like I'd left something behind.

* * * * *

I stayed at my desk late, crossing off each item from my to-do list as I went. It was around eight o'clock when Dean's door opened behind me. He didn't speak, so I turned and looked up at him.

"I'm glad you're still here," he said.

"Do you have another assignment for me?" I asked, trying not to sound hopeful.

He walked over and perched on the edge of my desk, looking down at me. "No. I just didn't want you to leave yet."

"I'll finish everything," I said. "I only have two things left."

He slid my to-do list across the desk and looked down at it. He balled it up and tossed it in the trash next to his feet.

"But—"

"I don't give a fuck about that right now."

I blinked at him, wondering if I'd done something wrong.

"Have dinner with me."

"Tonight?" I asked.

"Yes."

My eyes narrowed. "Did your other date back out?"

"Who?"

"The one you had last night?"

"Ah. That was an event, and I only took her because I couldn't show up alone. Truthfully, you were on my mind all night."

I swallowed. I couldn't have heard him right. How could someone like me be on *his* mind? My heart swelled. "I was?"

"Yes."

"What about all the stuff you said before about me being off limits?"

"It still applies. This is just dinner. No obligations. Consider it a thank you for this week."

I looked at the desk, picking at a black mark near the edge. I didn't want just dinner. I liked Dean. More than liked him. He was miles different from the boys my age, and suddenly, they didn't interest me. This man did.

"You seem disappointed," he said. "You know, even being Gary's daughter, I might—but you're so young…"

I looked up again. I waited, urging him to finish the sentence. What did I hope he'd say, though? I was going to get Trey back—I knew I could do it. So why did it matter what Dean thought?

"Anyway," he said. "Maybe dinner's not such a good idea after all. I've already hit my mistake quota for the day."

My face fell. "Earlier…you thought that was a mistake?"

"I've tasted something I shouldn't have, and now I'll suffer for it. You're just so damn beautiful."

I wilted back against my chair. "Me?"

"Doesn't he tell you that? Don't all the boys tell you that?"

"No," I whispered. "I don't think he ever did."

He shook his head. "Shame." He reached out and sifted strands of my blonde hair through his fingers.

"I want to," I said.

"Want to what?"

"Dinner."

He sighed heavily and dropped his hand, his eyes wandering around the room as he thought. He looked back at me. "Forget I said it. If I thought I could resist you, I would. But no, Alex. We can't have dinner. I never make the same mistake twice."

CHAPTER 8

It was like getting dumped all over again. Saturday I made the forty-minute drive to my parents' house in Calabasas because I needed a break. From the dorms, which held constant reminders of Trey. From the pristine office building I'd spent the last five days in. From Dean and the feeling of him buried inside me. He'd called it a mistake, but for me, it was just the opposite. I felt different from having known him intimately—and I now wanted things I didn't know existed before him.

My parents tried to get me to stay downstairs and talk, but all I wanted was to sleep in my own bed and forget the past month had ever happened. My nap lasted until after sundown, and when the smells of homemade cooking wafted upstairs to my bedroom, I changed into a plain sundress. I would've worn my pajama pants to dinner except that my mother always commented when I did.

Frank Sinatra crooned from the kitchen as I made my way downstairs, barefoot with my hair in a sloppy ponytail. Two glasses of wine and a tumbler of amber liquid came into view on the counter. My feet stopped. At the picturesque dining table sat Dean, handsome in a dress shirt, his normally rigid posture relaxed in his high-backed chair. He looked like he was posing for a magazine shoot.

My mother whirled around when she heard me enter. The clap of her hands was muted by oven mitts. "There's our girl," she said with a large smile.

My eyes were big as they fixed on Dean. "What are you doing here?"

"We've been inviting him by for years, and finally he agreed to come over for dinner. I really just can't recall the last time he was here."

Dean smiled slowly, a gleam in his eyes. "I figure it's the least they can do after sticking me with you for a week."

My mother giggled and shook her head. "Oh, Dean. You're awful."

"Of course I'm kidding," he said. "Working with your daughter was nothing but a pleasure."

My body was hot, even in my sundress. I wanted to melt onto the floor. I jumped when my dad touched my shoulder from behind.

"Looks like dinner's almost ready," he said. "Should we sit?"

My place setting was next to Dean and across from my parents. I sat down, still mildly in shock. Dean grinned at me like a schoolboy with a secret. When Dad stood to get their drinks, I snapped my head to Dean. "What are you doing here?"

"They invited me."

"But they invite you all the time."

"Mmm." He smiled, unruffled by my panic. "This time I had more reason to say yes than no."

"Me?" I couldn't even hide the desperation in my voice that I wanted to be the reason.

"I missed you, Alex. More than I thought possible in a twenty-four hour period."

"But you said—"

"And I maintain that. This is wrong. It can't happen. No touching—well, no *more* touching. But this way I get to see you, and I have no choice but to control myself."

"I—"

He looked forward again.

"What're you two whispering about?" my dad teased.

"No work at the dinner table," Mom said, setting down a dish of lasagna. She began dividing up pieces with a spatula. "But how was it? Did you two get along okay?"

We both nodded silently.

"Did you get your dress, honey?"

"Not yet," I said, picturing Dean's personal check still un-cashed in my purse. "Tomorrow, maybe."

"Well, we can't wait to see it."

I picked at my salad, half listening as they discussed the local real estate market and half ignoring Dean's unmistakable body heat. Trey and the group would be returning from Mexico sometime tonight, so my phone was tucked in one hidden pocket of my dress just in case. My attention returned fully to the conversation when my mom asked, "So, Dean, how are things with Cathy?"

My nostrils flared. *Cathy?*

"We're through," he said. "Have been for a few months now."

"Really?" I asked sharply.

He fixed a calm gaze on me and raised his eyebrows. "Yes, really."

"That's a shame," Dad said. "She seemed like a nice woman."

"Cathy?" I asked. "Who's Cathy?" I couldn't seem to stop saying her name.

Dean's hand unexpectedly landed on my thigh, and my body instantly relaxed at his touch. "She was a nice woman," he agreed, looking back at my dad. "But she's not what I'm looking for."

"So what're you looking for, Dean?" Mom asked. "Let us help. I'd really like to see you settle down with someone. It's been—how many years? Five? Since Amy—"

"I'd really rather not discuss it," Dean said.

"I think we should," I said through a dry throat. "Sounds kind of interesting."

His hand slid up my thigh, brushing under my dress like it was nothing. "I doubt that," he replied.

"You're just such a catch, and even in this community, there are so many women who…and I should've invited Vicky over for…loves lasagna, and her recipe for…"

My mom's voice faded away as Dean's fingers traced the line of my panties. I shook my head at my plate, but he squeezed my leg. My hand latched over his, pulling at it, telling him "no touching" without words. He wouldn't budge.

"I appreciate the thought, Deb," Dean said. "But really, I'm fine. You know how important work is to me."

"That's just because you don't have anyone."

One finger slipped into my underwear. My cheeks were fiery, my hand clenching around his wrist.

"Well, that's just not true. I have someone at this very moment."

My mom's eyes widened, and I had to look away. "Who?" she exclaimed.

His touch trailed along my slit. He pushed the tip of his finger into my wetness, massaging me softly.

"A girl I've been seeing."

"What's she like?"

"Smart. Witty. Good listener, hard-working, soaking."

"Soaking?" I choked out.

"*Smoking.* As in, she's smoking hot."

My mom wrinkled her nose. "*Smoking hot?* She sounds...young."

He grinned. He grabbed one of my hands with his free one and rested it on his hard crotch. "She is. I've got my hands full," he paused, driving his finger in deeper so I gasped, "and I love every minute of it."

He pulled away, stuck his finger in his mouth, and groaned. "Deb, your cooking is to die for."

My jaw dropped. I removed my hand and put it in my lap, pulling the hem of my dress.

"Well, thank you, Dean. I know how much you love your lasagna."

* * * * *

My parents cleared the dishes, finally giving Dean and I another moment alone.

"What was that?" I hissed. "What happened to staying in control? No touching?"

"Harder than I thought. But I'm not sorry, because that small taste was sweeter than any dessert."

"What?" I blushed and looked at my lap.

"Hey, Dean," my mom said. "How about some apple pie?"

"Actually, I have plans for dessert. I should take off anyway—it was a long week." He looked at me. "For both of us. Alexandra was just telling me she has to go back to campus tonight because she left her Sociology textbook in her room."

"But, Alex, you aren't taking Sociology," Dad said.

"It's...I—it's not. It's Biology."

"Alex," my mom said. "I hate the idea of you driving back at night."

"I'll follow her in my car," Dean said. He winked at me. "See she gets home safely."

"Is it important?" Dad asked. "Do you have homework?"

I swallowed and nodded. "Uh, yes? Yes. I have homework due on Monday."

Mom sighed, wiping down the counter. "Then you'd better get going. You really don't mind, Dean?"

"Not one bit. Happy to do it."

I ran upstairs to get my bag while Dean finished his drink with my dad. Once I'd gotten everything, I went at waited at the front door, feeling like a child with my duffel bag as Dean said goodnight to my parents.

After I got a hug and kiss from them both, they waved while Dean escorted me to my car.

"I won't be following you home," Dean said. "You'll be following me."

"Where?" I asked.

"To my apartment."

He glanced up at my parents, still standing under the yellow light of the porch. "I've decided I want you for my own tonight. Just one night, and then we can move on with our lives. Can you handle that, Alexandra?"

He didn't wait for my answer, just threw a casual wave at my parents as he walked away. I got in my car and drove out of the complex. Once we were out of my parents' sight, I pulled over, let Dean drive ahead, and blindly followed him back into the city.

* * * * *

I parked and turned off the ignition. I knew at any time I could've veered off, headed for home and left Dean to his sordid fantasies. But I didn't want that. His hands on me, under my skirt, smacking my ass— the thought alone drove me wild, making my foot weigh heavier on the gas pedal.

He tapped on my window, and I looked out at him. His handsome face was soft with a smile, his blue eyes deep but alive with something. Desire, maybe.

I got out. The slam of the driver's side door echoed around the underground parking garage. He stepped toward me until his body was long against mine, pressing me into the side of the car.

"You've never even kissed me," I said inches from his face.

I tilted my face upward, but he stopped me with a hand on each of my cheeks. "I'm not big on kissing," he said. "It reminds me of being in love."

I knew I should've been offended, but I just looked into his eyes, reading the reluctant pain there.

He pulled me closer and pecked me once. His lips pressed hard against mine for a moment. Finally, he opened his mouth. His hands slid back into my hair as our tongues met. The kiss grew heated and fast, steamrolling over us in an instant. I could taste his groan. His hands fell away and grasped my backside from the car, pulling me against him. I threw my head back, and he kissed his way up my throat, his heavy breathing hot on my skin.

"Inside," he rumbled. "Get inside now."

We walked briskly into his building, and the doorman greeted us. The elevator doors weren't even closed before he lifted me up by my ass and pinned me against the wall. His lips locked over mine, his hands pulling impatiently at the neckline of my dress. I squealed into his mouth as he gave up and shoved his hand in my bra, taking my nipple in his fingers.

"Tell me all the things you like," he breathed.

My already warm face flushed hotter. I had liked everything so far. He'd shown me things I hadn't even realized I *could* like. "What?"

"Tell me what you like so I can do it to you."

"I-I don't know…"

"Did you like your spanking?"

I nodded against him, and his hand underneath me squeezed my ass.

"What else?"

I was silently thankful when the doors split apart. I didn't know how to answer. I had practically no experience, a fact I'd only realized after Dean had had his way with me.

He set me on my feet and took my hand to lead me down the hall to a door. He pulled his keys from his pocket and glanced at me once. The smile he wore as he unlocked the door was the definition of sexy.

"After you," he said, gesturing for me to pass through.

The apartment was neutral, all grey, beige, black, and white. It was expansive though, and the view was mesmerizing. No woman had left any mark there, that much was obvious. I played with the flimsy strap of my cheap sundress.

"It's so nice," I said.

"You're so nice." I turned to face him, and his lips drew up in one corner.

He stuck his hands in his pockets. His shirt hung perfectly from his tall frame, and his jawline was darkening with fresh stubble. His charcoal hair was messy, but it only fueled my arousal knowing it was because of my hands.

I walked toward him. He took my wrist and brought my palm to his pants. He slid it up and down his cock.

"You have no idea how good that feels," he said when I closed my hand around the shape of him.

"I like this," I said. "And I liked when you made me crawl for you. I liked when you took me against the desk. I liked all of it."

He breathed in and out through his nose. "What did you like before that?"

"Nothing," I said immediately. "I think I was doing it wrong."

He laughed, but I didn't. With his other hand, he undid his button and pushed his pants down a little. He still had my wrist in an iron grip. He freed himself from his underwear next. I swallowed at the largeness of him. He replaced my hand there. Despite behind so hard, the skin was soft.

I wanted to be closer so I stepped until I came right under his chin. He bent his head and kissed me while I held his cock and his hand held my wrist. He guided it up and down, hissing into my mouth.

He let go of me to scrunch up my dress and put his hand between my legs. His other hand cupped the back of my head, fisting my hair gently. I gasped as his fingers found me wet, slipping inside me.

"How's that?" he asked.

I whispered and nodded my approval.

He pulled his fingers out and surprised me with a tight hug. He kissed me harder. My arms clung around his back.

He picked me up. My legs wrapped around his waist, and he kissed me even as we walked. He stopped long enough to look ahead and then again to drop me on my back on the bed. My dress slid over my head easily, and he tossed it aside. "Did you wear this for me?" he asked.

I looked down at the black lace bra and matching panties I'd changed into while upstairs gathering my things. "Of course."

He climbed onto the bed and kissed the curves of my breasts. He pulled one cup down, trussing me up for his mouth. I arched my back, clawing at the fabric of his dress shirt. He lifted to remove it and his undershirt by the collar.

I felt suddenly nervous in the hands of a man, so different from my experience with Trey. He had chest hair, defined, hard muscles, and faint lines around his eyes. He was the sexiest thing I'd ever seen. He stood from the bed and removed his pants the rest of the way, licking his lips as he did. He didn't glance down and around self-consciously the way Trey usually did—he looked at me like he was about to pull out silverware and have me for dessert.

"Stand up," he said.

I got to my feet in front of him.

"Turn around."

I did, keeping him in my sight with my head over my shoulder. "Good," he murmured, unclasping my bra. He leaned in and hugged me to his back, grasping my breasts. He kissed my cheek and dropped his hands to my panties. His fingers hooked in the elastic, and we both watched as he pulled them over my hips and dropped them at my ankles. His hardness pressed against my back as he sighed into my ear. His hands explored me leisurely, feeling between my legs, gliding along my wetness. When I couldn't stand it anymore, I turned in his embrace and touched his cheeks. I kissed him, and it wasn't long before we were falling back on the bed. I opened my legs to let him in when he pressed against me. He entered me slowly but firmly, pulling back every few seconds and thrusting a little deeper.

"Are you on birth control?" he asked as his pace increased.

"Yes," I breathed.

"Because I want to come inside you, Alexandra."

I nodded but said, "I thought you wanted to come on me."

"I did," he said with a small smile. "But that was before I wanted you as mine."

"Yours?" I repeated, stunned.

His smile fell, and he leaned into the curve of my neck, driving faster into me. The idea of being his made my entire body hot. My arms wrapped tightly around his neck, and my legs contracted around his waist. He picked me up, turned us around, and backed me up against the nearest wall. He was suddenly insatiable, bouncing me against it and nipping my earlobe. He held me up with one hand and the other wedged between us to find my sensitive clit. He rubbed it softly, but his fingers quickly grew firm and demanding. It pushed me over the edge and

I came all around him. He never stopped fucking me through it, nailing me to the wall over and over until he thrust deep and came for what felt like minutes, groaning in my ear while sliding in and out slowly. He bent his head and touched his lips to mine for a sweet, drawn-out kiss.

He didn't speak but pulled me from the wall and carried me into the bathroom before setting me on the counter. I looked around the lavish, marble space while he turned the faucet of the bathtub. He grabbed a bottle and poured liquid into the water.

"A bath?" I asked. "With bubbles?"

"You girls like bubble baths, don't you?"

I smiled. "Yes."

"Well, I like seeing you naked, so we both win."

I giggled and crossed my arms, suddenly shy.

He shook his head while holding his hand under the stream of water. "Please—*please* do not ever cover yourself up in front of me. It's offensive."

My face reddened, but my smile grew. I let my arms fall away, thinking I'd never met anyone as straightforward as him. He left the water running and walked to the door. "Want a drink?" he asked.

"I'm underage."

"As if I could forget. Can you pretend to be an adult tonight?"

I stuck out my bottom lip, and he laughed.

"Or don't," he said.

"I'll have what you're having."

I sighed happily to myself over what had just happened, waiting for him. Who knew it could be that good? *Who knew?*

Dean reentered the bathroom and walked directly to me, setting two glasses on the counter. He slid my hips forward so we fit perfectly together. "Red wine for you," he murmured. "I didn't think you'd care for scotch."

"I've never tasted it," I said.

"No?" He brought his drink to his lips and took a sip. He leaned in and licked his tongue over mine.

"I think I like it." I tried for more. "A lot," I added.

He bent me backward over his forearm and kissed me more excitedly.

"You sure do kiss a lot for not being big on it," I said.

"I'm getting the feeling it has more to do with who I'm kissing than anything."

We looked at each other until my eyes widened. "The bath."

He turned and twisted the knob just in time, but when he climbed in and sat, water sloshed over the side.

"Open that drawer under your legs," he said.

"You can't tell me what to do anymore."

"Technically you're mine for the week, and…if I'm not mistaken, it's Saturday night."

"That was only until Friday."

"You sure about that? Where in our contract did it say Friday?"

My brows furrowed. "There was no contract."

"Then it's my word against yours. And since I'm the boss…"

I rolled my eyes playfully.

He winked as I hopped down from the counter to open the drawer. I surveyed the contents. "Cigars?" I asked.

I selected one and picked a few more things from the drawer. I left our drinks behind and sat in the bath across from him while holding my hands above water.

"Can I cut it for you?" I asked.

"I've never let anyone cut my cigar before."

I smiled and held it over the bathtub's ledge.

"How do you know how to do that?" he asked as I positioned the guillotine.

"Dad taught me." I chopped it in one motion. I held it to my lips, lit it, then handed it to him.

He raised his eyebrows. "I might be impressed."

I shrugged. "So, what would the office say if they knew I was in a bath with Mr. Brittany?"

He laughed.

"Have, um…?"

"Yes?" he prompted.

"Have any of them taken a bath with Mr. Brittany?"

"I told you how I feel about interoffice relationships."

"I know, but you broke that rule pretty quickly with me."

"I'm aware."

"Is it because I was a temp?"

"It's because you're you."

I grinned. "You know, when you're not the boss, you can be sort of romantic. But don't worry, I won't tell anyone."

He smiled too and rested his head against the back of the tub. I watched him smoke with his eyes closed for a while. I'd thought he was handsome before, but now he was irresistible. I couldn't understand how I was the one sitting there between his legs. Weren't there women of all ages falling all over him? "That was an interesting conversation at dinner," I said, trying to sound casual when actually I was fishing for information.

"Which one?" he asked.

"About you and Cathy."

He grunted. "What're you getting at?"

"I'm just wondering why you're still single. I mean," I paused, swallowing, "you are, aren't you? When you said you were seeing someone—"

"Of course I was talking about you," he said. "It was all in good fun."

"Oh. Okay."

He raised an eyebrow and opened his eyes. "If I had a girlfriend, she'd be sitting where you are right now. I'm not the type to fuck around."

I looked down at his tone. "Good," I said. "I'm glad to hear that."

He closed his eyes again and continued smoking. I watched him, wondering what nerve I'd struck. Wondering why I didn't want this night to end. Finally, he set down his cigar. "Do you want to go home tonight?" he asked.

I shifted against the back of the tub. "I will if you want me to."

He lifted his head. "That wasn't the question."

I looked around the bathroom, chewing on the inside of my lip. It was the last thing I wanted. I knew I was getting into dangerous territory, but it was our only night together. "No," I said after a moment. "I don't want to."

"Then you'll stay the night."

I nodded. "Okay."

He stood up from the water. I blinked away quickly, reddening because it put me face to face with his cock. He grabbed two towels from the nearest rack and handed me one. I followed him into the bedroom and to the bed.

From behind, he stripped my towel away and kissed my shoulder. He squatted down. Before I could turn my head over my shoulder, he pushed me forward so I was folded over the bed. He licked me softly between the legs, and my body shuddered.

"Did he do this for you?" Dean asked.

"Yes," I whispered.

"Then the poor bastard knows what he's missing. How wonderful you taste. Soapy. And sweet."

His tongue became more insistent, harder. Flatter. Then demanding again. I pushed my forehead into the mattress, welcoming each flick that brought me closer to where I wanted to be.

He stood up and closed himself over my back. His cock sank into me from behind, a perfect fit. I moaned into the bed, my teeth biting the comforter. I felt his hand in my long hair, wrapping it around his wrist, urging me backward. His lips sought mine, so I turned my head to give him what he wanted. His hips rammed faster into me, my hair still firm in his grip.

"I'm going to pull your hair, and you're going to come," he said, barely moving his mouth from mine.

"Yes," I said.

He kissed me again, the corner of my mouth, snaking his tongue along my teeth. He pulled my hair hard so my head flew back in the same moment his thrusts became relentless.

"That's good, Alexandra," he said. It wasn't just the drive of his hard cock that ignited my orgasm but the way he controlled my body. "Come for me. Fuck, I'm about to come too."

My orgasm was less intense than the one before, but it lasted longer. I was still shuddering under him as he emptied himself in me. He lay heavy on top of me as we caught our breath.

"Dean," I breathed. "Mr. Brittany."

"Yes, Alex?" He kissed my cheek, then over my hair. "Miss James?"

"I can't believe you fingered me in front of my parents."

He laughed in a burst of air against my cheek. "It was just a sample. God, and I was so fucking hard."

I smiled. "Yes, I know."

He lifted himself up and drew back the sheets of the bed. I crawled in beside him, melting when he pulled my body securely to his side. I placed my cheek on his chest. Heard his heartbeat. I was sated, but there was a hole growing in me as I thought of leaving him the next day. And it diminished my satisfaction. The more I got, the more I needed, as if Dean were my personal brand of drug.

"Earlier in the bathtub," I said, "you sounded angry when I asked if you were seeing anyone."

He hummed, his chest vibrating. "Yeah. What was with the questions about other women?"

"I just—I know you divorced from Amy a few years ago—"

"Five."

"Okay, five. Why haven't you remarried? Why don't you have a girlfriend?"

His torso rose and fell with a sigh. "Amy cheated on me."

I grimaced. Cheating on someone like Dean seemed inherently wrong—and a little scary. He wasn't the type to take that lying down. "I'm sorry. Dad never mentioned that."

"Since then, I haven't really had the desire to fully commit to anyone else."

My lips pressed into a line. "That's not really fair. You shouldn't let her ruin love for you like that."

"That's a good attitude," he said as if he were trying not to laugh. "Naïve, but a good one nonetheless."

"Naïve?" I balked.

"Marriage doesn't run solely on love. There are many other things that factor in."

"But you and Amy seemed happy. At least I remember it that way."

"We were. I loved her, and when I found out what was going on, it hurt. But we went through therapy, and I learned the reasons behind it. I worked too much, didn't pay enough attention to her or anything in our lives. I was in the city five days a week for work, and some nights I wouldn't even have the energy to make the drive home, so I got this apartment. She felt neglected. She thought maybe I saw other women when I slept here—I never did. We finally started communicating."

"Then why'd you divorce?"

"Like I said, it's not just about love. Our marriage was too damaged at that point. We tried for a few months, but she'd lost my trust completely, and on top of that, I blamed myself."

He was different while he spoke. Human. After being so rigid this week, his vulnerability was not only welcome, but attractive. I hugged him closer to me, and he ran a hand over my hair.

"So I've spilled my guts," he said. "You know more about my relationship with my ex-wife than most. How about you? Why don't you tell me about this boy?"

Boy? It seemed so long ago now. Had I been crying over him just a few days earlier? "I'm naked in bed with you. Wouldn't that be weird?"

"No. Go ahead. Who is this kid?"

"Trey," I said. "I met him at orientation, and we ended up in the same dorm. We've been dating since around Thanksgiving."

"Has he met your parents?"

I shook my head. "He was going to this summer."

"Where is he now?"

"Mexico. We were all going for Spring Break, but I backed out last minute." I shrugged. "He said he wouldn't go if I did, and the thought of drinking and partying all week without him didn't sound like fun."

"So you think this dress is the answer to all your problems?"

I nodded. "I look amazing in it."

"I'll be honest, you looked amazing in pea-green. If he can't see that, he doesn't deserve you."

My lashes fluttered. "Thank you, but—"

"No but. You are beautiful. Learn to take a compliment."

I flushed, unable to contain my smile. I looked up at him in the light of the bedside lamp and sneakily admired his strong nose and the line of his jaw. I was tempted to tell him he was beautiful too.

Instead, I closed my eyes. A moment later, he shifted against me to shut off the lamp, and then I was floating in his clean, male scent, drifting off in this new bed in new arms.

CHAPTER 9

I awoke curled against Dean's chest. When I looked up, he was reading a newspaper intently.

"Dean?"

He glanced down. "Morning."

"You've already been up?"

"Just to get the paper and coffee." He smiled. "You're a heavy sleeper."

I nodded and yawned.

He kissed the top of my head. "How'd you sleep?"

"Really well. Thank you."

"Anytime," he said with a low chuckle. I let my eyes wander down over his skin and the chest hair that covered it. I touched him gently with my fingers.

"What're your plans today?" he asked, still reading.

I beamed up at him. "Just to get my dress."

"When's the formal?"

"Next weekend."

He rubbed my back, the newspaper crinkling as he set it down. "You'll have all the guys at your feet."

"I only need one." My smile wavered with his frown. Did he want to be that one? Did I want that? It could never work, and I chastised myself for being so stupid as to spend the night with him. It made everything too real. "I guess I should get going."

He sat forward, so I did too. "Not yet. First, breakfast. Then I'll let you go."

"Okay," I said, brightening at the thought of spending more time with him.

He gave me a t-shirt to wear as he pulled on pajama pants. He cooked a breakfast of bacon and eggs. I watched. He was relaxed. I liked that version of him. I admitted to myself I also liked the other version, the non-relaxed, rigid man—more than I probably should have.

After we ate, I insisted on doing the dishes, but he waved me away. He cleaned, and I returned to his room to change into jeans I had packed for my parents' house.

I tucked hair behind my ear, watching as he dried his hands with a dishtowel. The more comfortable I became with him—with the idea of him, a man more than twice my age who moved like he owned the world—the more attracted I was to him. He turned around, and I smiled.

"Thanks," I said. "For everything. My spring break went way better than I thought."

"And," he said, "you're getting a new dress out of it."

I loved the dress. I could almost feel it in my hands. But at that moment, it seemed completely insignificant. I smoothed out my furrowed eyebrows and nodded. "A new dress," I repeated. "Sure."

"I'll walk you out."

In the doorway, I turned to face him. He leaned against the molding, crossing his bare, brawny arms and looking down at me. "Good luck at the formal. If you ever need anything—a job, whatever—call."

I cleared my throat. I didn't want to leave without a kiss, but I was afraid to make a move. I waited until it became awkward and then finally turned. He caught my wrist and pulled me back. He drew me against his chest, and his other hand cupped the back of my head. "And if you ever need *me*, call."

"You?" I asked, searching his eyes.

"I'd tell you to stay, but it wouldn't be fair to you. It wouldn't be right." He lowered his lips, hovering above me. "It would be selfish of me, and very, very wrong." He kissed me gently. I meant to respond, but my mind melted when our mouths opened to each other. My arms went around his neck and brought him closer. He kissed me in a way I'd never been kissed before. I was scared for it to end, and when it did, I almost pulled him back.

His bottomless blue eyes spoke, but his mouth remained in a closed line. He looked away and returned into the apartment, closing the door behind him.

I remained there, stunned for a moment, acutely feeling the loss of him. Eventually I made it to the elevator and eventually, I drove home.

CHAPTER 10

Gold sequins shimmered into my world, blinding me even from across the store. The dress sat simply on the hanger, calling to me. I clutched Dean's check in one hand, approaching the dress like a piece of artwork. The bank was a couple blocks down, but I couldn't bring myself to cash it just yet. For some reason, it felt like the end of Dean and me. But had anything even started? Could what we had even end?

I looked from the check to the dress and back. I ran my hand down the sleeve, my fingers skipping along the small sequins.

"It's beautiful, isn't it?"

I turned to the sales associate.

"Unfortunately, it's our last one," she said, reaching out and taking the hanger, "and it's already been sold."

I gaped at her, my eyes pleading. "Wait—what? B-but, you don't understand. I *need* this dress."

She shook her head. "I'm sorry. Unless your name is Alexandra and you're a size four, this one's taken."

My eyes widened. "My name *is* Alexandra."

She winked. "Then I suppose this dress is yours."

"I don't understand."

"I just got off the phone with a Mr. Brittany. He said you'd be by—that is, if you're the beautiful, young blonde named Alexandra."

I raised my eyebrows. "Yes. That's me, apparently."

She smiled. "Then I'll wrap this up for you."

"But how did he know?"

"He said you'd ask that. Apparently he's a powerful man with many connections, and one little gold dress doesn't stand a chance against him. I think he asked your mom."

I shook my head, my lips spreading into a disbelieving smile.

The saleswoman placed the dress in a box, tied a ribbon around it and handed it to me in a sturdy shopping bag.

"Wherever you're going in this, I hope it's special," she said. "Because this is a very special dress."

It was a special dress, meant for a special event and a special person. Trey—he'd been special once, but I wasn't so sure anymore. No, this wasn't just any dress, and even she knew it.

* * * * *

The bathroom door rattled as the knocking became more impatient. "Come on, Alex," Chad yelled from my room. "We already missed all the pre-gaming. Seriously. The formal started an hour ago."

"Okay," I called back. I swung the door open and spun.

"Holy shit," Chad said. "That dress was worth every penny."

"I told you," I said, squealing.

"Okay. You were right. Trey will be putty in your hands."

I nodded excitedly. "Does he know you're bringing me?"

"Nah. I thought it'd be better to surprise him."

"Good. That's good."

"Our deal's still on, right?"

"Yes. Tonight, my life's mission—other than mending my broken heart, of course—is distracting Todd so you can finally talk to Elyse."

"I meant what I said, Alex. Todd may be my frat brother, but she deserves much better than that prick. He's just trying to get in her pants."

"Todd's an asshole," I agreed. "Otherwise I wouldn't butt in."

"Cool." His face fell. "But I'm serious, we're really fucking late."

I laughed. "Fine. Grab my purse, would you?"

He disappeared into the room and I gave my reflection one last look. My blonde hair fell in soft curls over my shoulders, and my makeup was heavier than usual, but not so much that it was overdone. After all, I wanted the dress to stand out.

The dress—it fit perfectly. I wasn't sure how Dean knew my size, but he was dead on. It was fitted, pulling in tightly at the waist and curving over my hips. It stopped a few inches above my knees. The sleeves came just below my elbows and the back dipped so low that I couldn't wear a bra. Most girls would be wearing dresses that made them feel sexy, that made the guys feel sexy. But I wanted something different—I wanted Trey to fall in love with me all over again.

* * * * *

Chad looped his arm in mine. "Ready?"

I took a deep breath. "Yes."

He pulled open the door to the hotel's ballroom, and the music went from muted to loud and pulsing. The room was softly lit, and Chad had to lean in when he asked if I wanted a drink. I nodded as I scanned the crowd, my hair bouncing. He disappeared, and I headed for a group of my friends in the corner. They were talking about Mexico—

again—as though they hadn't been all week. I smiled and laughed along as I had been, listening to stories I really didn't care about. Something had felt off since they'd returned last weekend, as if they as people just weren't as interesting, but I'd figured it was my nerves acting up. I hadn't seen Trey once.

Chad returned with a rum and Coke for each of us, and I stuck the straw between my teeth, drinking quickly.

"Whoa, slow down there," Chad teased.

I made a face. "I'm nervous."

He rubbed my back. "I know. Don't be. You look amazing."

I nodded and just then, my eyes met Trey's across the room. He looked at Chad and then back at me, his eyebrows knitting. I glanced up at Chad and laughed.

"What?" he asked.

"Nothing," I said through a large smile. I clamped my teeth together and said, "He's looking over here."

"Oh. But so is Elyse."

My eyes widened. "Shit."

He laughed too and shrugged. "Maybe it's working in both our favors."

I handed him my drink with my eyes on Trey. "I'm going to talk to him."

Chad bumped his shoulder into mine. "Good luck, gorgeous."

Everything seemed to slow as I made my way across the ballroom. Even the music faded out for a quieter song. The crowd parted. Trey looked at me and nothing else. It was perfect. He stuck a hand in his pocket and scratched his head with the other, ruffling his blond hair.

"Hey," he said when I was close.

"Hi."

"Didn't know you'd be here."

I shrugged. "Is it a bad thing?"

"No," he said immediately. "I'm glad."

"Are you here with anyone?"

He nodded over my shoulder, but I didn't look. "Tiff from our dorm."

"Oh."

"It's not like you think. It was just a last-minute thing. I mean, I wasn't expecting—anyway, you look really…did you get a haircut or something?"

I shook my head. "Not since the last time we saw each other. You know, the day you dumped me."

He glanced at the floor. "Yeah." He looked up over his shoulder and back at me. "What's the deal with Chad? You here with him?"

"Maybe."

"Would he care if we danced?"

I held my arms open, and his slipped around me. His cologne was familiar as I put my cheek against his. Dean's arms when he'd picked me up were solid, like they'd never, ever drop me. Trey's, on the other hand, rested limply around my waist.

"How was Mexico?" I asked.

He shrugged. "It was cool. Lots of drinking."

"Did you hook up with anyone?"

He laughed near my ear. "Geez, Alex. We were broken up."

"Were?"

"Yeah, I hooked up with a couple girls. No one in our group, just girls from other schools."

"Oh."

"But it made me miss you."

"Oh?"

"Yeah. Like, you're…different—from them."

My heart sped. It was what I'd been hoping for for weeks. I almost couldn't believe the dress had actually worked, as if I'd been clinging to some false hope all along. "What're you saying, Trey?"

He pulled back and looked between us at our feet. "So are you here with Chad or not?"

I shook my head.

"Maybe we could go somewhere and talk," he said. "I got a room upstairs."

"For you and Tiff?" I asked, stepping away.

"No, no," he said, grasping my forearm and coaxing me back. "Just, like, to have it. Just in case."

My eyes narrowed on me. "Okay," I said hesitantly. I wanted that time with him, even if it was meant for someone else. "Let's go."

"Great." He kissed me on the cheek. His hand slid into mine. We walked to the elevator, and he fished in his back pocket for the keycard.

"I know I said I wanted space," he said. We watched the numbers tick off as we ascended. "But obviously I still love you."

The elevator doors opened with a ding. I followed him to the room, clutching my purse, walking behind him slightly.

One of his frat brothers, Duncan, appeared around the corner and barreled toward us.

"Richards," he yelled belligerently. "You bastard. It's not even nine o'clock, and you're already getting some ass."

Trey's laugh echoed through the otherwise quiet hallway. He slid the keycard from the slot and pushed the door open. "Fuck off, D. This is my girlfriend."

Duncan nodded at me, his body wavering. "No shit, you think I don't know Alex? Listen, you two, make sure you use protection. Think I got a—" His eyes went blurry as he patted his pockets. "Got a Trojan or something—"

Trey rolled his eyes. "Dude. It's a frat party. You think I don't have condoms? I'm not a fucking idiot."

I frowned. The thought of him with Tiff or even other girls in Mexico made my stomach churn. Obviously he hadn't given me a second thought while I'd been here, pining away, working my freshly-slapped ass off so I could win him back.

Duncan pointed at Trey. "You still owe me a drink, you bastard."

"The drinks are free."

"I don't give a fuck. You owe me."

"Fine," Trey said, laughing again. "We'll see you downstairs in a little bit."

Trey ushered me into the room. He fumbled for the light switch, then seemed to change his mind and headed for the lamp, turning on the single low light. I watched him as he ran a hand through his hair.

"You didn't miss much in Mexico," he said. "Just a lot of that kind of shit."

I imagined several Duncans and Treys running around the dingy bars, sand raining from their hair while they danced with girls in skimpy tops.

He crossed the room to me and swept my hair over my shoulder. He finally looked me in the eyes long and hard. There was something missing from that look, but it was no different than any look he'd ever given me. It hit me that it wasn't the way I wanted to be looked at—and that maybe I'd been wrong these last couple weeks about what I needed.

He leaned in and touched his lips to mine.

"What are you doing?" I asked.

"I don't know. You look so good. I just felt like kissing you."

"We came up here to talk."

"Come on. You're not that naïve."

No, I wasn't. I knew why I was there. I sighed deeply and ran my hands over his biceps. "Does this mean we're back together?"

He rested his forehead against mine. "Yeah. Let's try this again, Alex. If you want."

He kissed me harder this time, pressing his tongue between my lips. He tasted minty and cool, and a little like beer. My eyebrows wrinkled as his arms tightened around my waist, his tongue delving deeper.

I needed more. I stepped back from him and turned around. He unzipped the dress halfway, and I wiggled my backside.

"What are you doing?" he asked.

"Touch me," I said.

"I am."

"Lower."

His hands moved down and stopped. "What do you want me to do?"

"What do *you* want to do?"

"Um." He rubbed the curve of my ass, then squeezed. "Jesus, this dress is scratchy."

"Spank me," I said suddenly, growing frustrated. "Please? Would you spank me?"

"Uh. No?"

I glared at him over my shoulder.

"Yes?" he corrected. "You want me to?"

"Why else would I ask?"

"It's just…you've never asked me to—you don't even like when I pull your hair."

"I don't?"

"I did once. You told me to told me to stop."

I was searching my memory when his palm landed gently on my ass cheek. I looked over my shoulder at him.

He was laughing silently. "I'm sorry," he said. "This just doesn't seem like you."

I straightened my back and turned around, crossing my arms. "It's a new dress," I said, glancing down. "That's what's different."

"Yeah, it's a nice dress. Really...shiny. I told you, you look good. More than good."

"More than good?" I repeated, cringing.

He threw up his arms. "What do you want from me? I thought you wanted to get back together. You were pissed when we broke up. Your roommate told me you cried for days."

I nodded. "You're right. This is exactly what I wanted." I looked down at my dress again. If I listened hard, I could still hear the music thumping from the ground floor. Here was Trey, wanting to make me whole again. But somewhere over the past two weeks, I'd already put myself back together. Or someone else had.

"Dean," I said softly.

"What?" Trey asked.

"I have to go," I said, turning away.

"Alex—wait."

I walked to the hotel room door and then paused. I looked back at Trey.

"I'm sorry," he said. "I was wrong. I shouldn't have broken up with you, and I shouldn't have told you about those other girls. Really—I want this."

"No, you don't," I said. "You want the dress. But I need someone who wants me with or without it."

The heavy door *whooshed* when I opened it. An audible click was all I heard behind me—not Trey's footsteps or his words attempting to stop me.

Once I hit the lobby, I strode toward the exit. When I spotted my friend Elyse with Todd, I hurried over, touching her arm.

"Hey, Al—"

"You know my date?" I asked, pointing toward the ballroom.

She squinted her eyes even though the door was closed. "You mean Chad?"

"Yeah." I glanced at Todd and back at her. "He told me you're the most beautiful girl here tonight."

Her eyes softened. "Really?"

"No. He said you were the most beautiful girl he'd ever seen—but he told me that on Monday when we were hanging outside of the English building, and you walked by and waved."

"I was hungover that day." She cringed. "And I wore my pajamas to class. I didn't even brush my hair."

"Exactly."

I walked away, hoping that was enough, because I was a week late already. Out in the cool night, I breathed in the fresh air and hailed a cab.

"Where to?" the cabby asked once I was inside.

I sat back in my seat. On a Friday night—where would Dean be? I gave him an address and smoothed my hair down as we pulled away from the curb.

When we arrived, I absentmindedly paid the cab driver, my thoughts coming fast. I waved my building pass, still dangling from my keychain, at the security guard. In the elevator, I wrung my fingers in front of me. My nerves flared with each floor I passed. The doors opened to complete and silent darkness.

I stepped out and went to Dean's office. It was seconds before I heard the tapping of fingers against a keyboard. An older woman glanced up, her eyes scanning over me.

"Um, we're closed for business right now," she said. "Can I help you?"

I stuck out my hand. "You must be Grace. I'm Alexandra, the—"

"Of course," she said, standing and taking my hand. "The temp. Thank you for your help last week—was there a problem with the check?"

"No. I'm here to see Mr. Brittany."

The door opened just then and Dean leaned against the frame. His hair was disheveled and there were bags under his eyes as if he hadn't been sleeping well, but he looked as handsome as he had moments before he'd shut his apartment door and left me in the hallway.

He didn't seem surprised to see me. "Grace, go home for the night, please."

"Oh." She nodded after a moment, gathering her things as we stared at each other. When she'd left, he turned and walked back into his office, leaving the door open.

"What are you doing here, Alex?"

I stopped in the doorway, mustering all my courage. "What do you think?"

He stood behind his desk and shook his head. "I think there's no way the boy turned you down looking like that."

"You're right," I said.

He placed just his fingertips on the surface of the desk. "Then, again, I ask—why are you here?"

I needed to feel him. I shifted on my feet, fighting the urge to run into his arms. "I don't know," I said softly.

"You got what you wanted."

"Yes. I did. But it's not what I want anymore."

"We can't, Alexandra. It would never work."

"It would," I said. "This is what I want."

"You should go." He turned his back to me. "You're too young. Gary—he'd never understand. And college is the time for…it doesn't matter. Just—go."

I swallowed, at a loss for words. I didn't know I wanted this but suddenly I couldn't live without it—without *him*. In his perfect suit, he was commanding and broad, but his shoulders fell slightly. Without thinking, I dropped to the floor on my hands and knees. I tossed my pursed aside, and he turned at the noise it made.

"What are you doing?"

I crawled slowly to his desk, never removing my eyes from him. He watched, motionless, until I was at his feet.

"Go back to him, Alexandra."

"How can I?" I asked, tears threatening. I was overwhelmed, not just from the fact that I wanted him, but with how badly I did. And how stupid I'd been to think I'd actually missed Trey, when that hadn't even scratched the surface of how much I'd missed Dean. "How can I possibly go back to Trey now—or anyone else for that matter?"

"You have to. Our lives are too different, and you need someone your own age."

"I don't," I said. "That week changed me."

He swallowed, looking down and shaking his head. But I could see his eyes giving into me.

"Yours," I said.

"You never cashed the check."

"I want to be yours—not just for a week."

"Mine," he repeated and sighed. "Get off the floor."

"No."

"Excuse me?"

"Not until you tell me yes. Not until you say—"

"You're mine," he said.

I stood and stepped under his chin. "I don't care if it's wrong. I don't care what they say. Make me yours, and none of that matters."

He grasped my cheeks and pulled me close to his lips. He kissed me ravenously, and my entire body

103

wilted against him. Sturdy arms caught me, holding me upright as he consumed me.

"I hope you're ready to stay," he said. "When you walked out of my apartment last weekend, it took all my willpower not to pull you back in. And that's the last time I'll ever fight that urge."

I touched his cheek and smiled, my heart expanding in my chest.

"And you were right," he continued, his hand trailing down my back to rest on my zipper. "You look amazing in this dress. But let's get you out of it."

CONNECT
WITH JESSICA

Stay updated & join the
JESSICA HAWKINS Mailing List
www.JESSICAHAWKINS.net/mailing-list

www.amazon.com/author/jessicahawkins
www.facebook.com/jessicahawkinsauthor
twitter: @jess_hawk
www.pinterest.com/jhauthor
instagram: @thecityscapeseries

ABOUT THE AUTHOR

JESSICA HAWKINS grew up between the purple mountains and under the endless sun of Palm Springs, California. She studied international business at Arizona State University and has also lived in Costa Rica and New York City. Some of her favorite things include traveling, her dog Kimo, Scrabble, driving aimlessly and creating Top Five lists. She is the helpless victim of an overactive imagination that finds inspiration in music and tranquility in writing. Currently she resides wherever her head lands, which lately is the unexpected (but warm) keyboard of her trusty MacBook.

Made in the USA
Charleston, SC
12 March 2015